A
Soul
in a
Bottle

A Soul in a Bottle

Tim Powers

Illustrated by J. K. Potter

Subterranean Press 2006

First Edition

Limited Edition ISBN
1-59606-074-3

Trade Hardcover ISBN
1-59606-075-1

Subterranean Press
PO Box 190106
Burton, MI 48519

www.subterraneanpress.com

To Algis Budrys
excellent writer, teacher and friend

THE FORECOURT OF the Chinese Theater smelled of rain-wet stone and car-exhaust, but a faint aroma like pears and cumin seemed to cling to his shirt-collar as he stepped around the clustered tourists, who all appeared to be blinking up at the copper towers above the forecourt wall or smiling into cameras as they knelt to press their hands into the puddled hand-prints in the cement paving blocks.

George Sydney gripped his shopping bag under his arm and dug three pennies from his pants pocket.

For the third of fourth time this morning he found himself glancing sharply over his left shoulder, but again there was no one within yards of him. The morning sun was bright on the Roosevelt Hotel across the boulevard, and the clouds were breaking up in the blue sky.

He crouched beside Jean Harlow's square and carefully laid one penny in each of the three round indentations below her incised signature, then wiped his wet fingers on his jacket. The coins wouldn't stay there long, but Sydney always put three fresh ones down whenever he walked past this block of Hollywood Boulevard.

He straightened up and again caught

a whiff of pears and cumin, and when he glanced over his left shoulder there was a girl standing right behind him.

At first glance he thought she was a teenager—she was a head shorter than him, and her tangled red hair framed a narrow, freckled face with squinting eyes and a wide, amused mouth.

"*Three* pennies?" she asked, and her voice was deeper than he would have expected.

She was standing so close to him that his elbow had brushed her breasts when he'd turned around.

"That's right," said Sydney, stepping back from her, awkwardly so as not to scuff the coins loose.

"Why?"

"Uh…" He waved at the cement square and then barely caught his shopping bag. "People pried up the original three," he said. "For souvenirs. That she put there. Jean Harlow, when she put her hand-prints and shoe-prints in the wet cement, in 1933."

The girl raised her faint eyebrows and blinked down at the stone. "I never knew that. How did you know that?"

"I looked her up one time. Uh, on Google."

The girl laughed quietly, and in that moment she seemed to be the only figure in the forecourt, including himself, that had color. He realized dizzily that the scent he'd been catching all morning was hers.

"Google?" she said. "Sounds like a Chinaman trying to say something. Are you always so nice to dead people?"

Her black linen jacket and skirt were visibly damp, as if she had slept outside, and seemed to be incongruously formal.

He wondered if somebody had donated the suit to the Salvation Army place down the boulevard by Pep Boys, and if this girl was one of the young people he sometimes saw in sleeping bags under the marquee of a closed theater down there.

"Respectful, at least," he said, "I suppose."

She nodded. "'Lo,'" she said, "'some we loved, the loveliest and the best…'"

Surprised by the quote, he mentally recited the next two lines of the Rubaiyat quatrain—*That Time and Fate of all their Vintage prest,/ Have drunk their cup a round or two before*—and found himself saying the last line out loud: "'And one by one crept silently to Rest.'"

She was looking at him intently, so he cleared his throat and said, "Are you local? You've been here before, I gather." Probably that odd scent was popular right now, he thought, the way patchouli oil had apparently been in the '60s. Probably he had brushed past someone who had been wearing it too, earlier in the day.

"I'm staying at the Heroic," she said, then went on quickly, "Do you live near here?"

He could see her bra through her damp white blouse, and he looked away—though he had noticed that it seemed to be embroidered with vines.

"I have an apartment up on Franklin," he said, belatedly.

She had noticed his glance, and arched her back for a moment before pulling her jacket closed and buttoning it. "'And in a Windingsheet of Vineleaf wrapped,'" she said merrily, "'So bury me by some sweet Gardenside.'"

Embarrassed, he muttered the first line of that quatrain: "'Ah, with the grape my fading life provide...'"

"Good idea!" she said—then she frowned, and her face was older. "No, dammit, I've got to go—but I'll see you again, right? I like you." She leaned forward and tipped her face up—and then she had briefly kissed him on the lips, and he did drop his shopping bag.

When he had crouched to pick it up and brushed the clinging drops of cold water off on his pants, and looked around, she was gone. He took a couple of steps toward the theater entrance, but the dozens of colorfully dressed strangers blocked his view, and he couldn't tell if she had hurried inside; and he didn't see her among the people by the photo booths or on the shiny black sidewalk.

Her lips had been hot—perhaps she had a fever.

He opened the plastic bag and peered inside, but the book didn't seem to have got wet or landed on a corner. A first edition of Colleen Moore's *Silent Star*, with a TLS, a typed letter, signed, tipped in on the front flyleaf. The Larry Edmunds Bookstore a few blocks east was going to give him fifty dollars for it.

And he thought he'd probably stop at Boardner's afterward and have a couple of beers before walking back to his apartment. Or maybe a shot of Wild Turkey, though it wasn't yet noon. He knew he'd be coming back here again, soon, frequently—peering around, lingering, almost certainly uselessly.

Still, *I'll see you again*, she had said. *I like you.*

Well, he thought with a nervous smile as he started east down the black sidewalk, stepping around the inset brass-rimmed pink stars with names on them, I like you too. Maybe, after all, it's a rain-damp street girl that I can fall in love with.

She wasn't at the Chinese Theater when he looked for her there during the next several days, but a week later he saw her again. He was driving across Fairfax on Santa Monica Boulevard, and he saw her standing on the side-walk in front of the big Starbuck's, in the shadows below the aquamarine openwork dome.

He knew it was her, though she was

wearing jeans and a sweatshirt now—her red hair and freckled face were unmistakable. He honked the horn as he drove through the intersection, and she looked up, but by the time he had turned left into a market parking lot and driven back west on Santa Monica, she was nowhere to be seen.

He drove around several blocks, squinting as the winter sunlight shifted back and forth across the streaked windshield of his ten-year-old Honda, but none of the people on the sidewalks was her.

A couple of blocks south of Santa Monica he passed a fenced-off motel with plywood over its windows and several shopping carts in its otherwise empty parking lot. The 1960s space-age sign over the building read RO IC MOTEL, and he could see faint outlines where a long-gone T and P had once made "tropic" of the first word.

"Eroic," he said softly to himself.

To his own wry embarrasment he parked a block past it and fed his only quarter into the parking meter, but at the end of his twenty minutes she hadn't appeared.

Of course she hadn't. "You're acting like a high-school kid," he whispered impatiently to himself as he put the Honda in gear and pulled away from the curb.

Six days later he was walking east toward Book City at Cherokee, and as was his habit lately he stepped into the Chinese Theater forecourt with three pennies in his hand, and he stood wearily beside the souvenir shop and scanned the crowd, shaking the pennies in his fist. The late afternoon crowd consisted of brightly-dressed tourists, and a portly, bearded man making hats out of balloons, and several young men dressed as Batman and Spiderman and Captain Jack Sparrow from the *Pirates of the Caribbean* movies.

Then he gripped the pennies tight. He saw her.

She was at the other end of the crowded square, on the far side of the theater entrance, and he noticed her red hair in the moment before she crouched out of sight.

He hurried through the crowd to where she was kneeling—the rains had passed and the pavement was dry—and he saw that she had laid three pennies into little round indentations in the Gregory Peck square.

She grinned up at him, squinting in the sunlight. "I love the idea," she said in the remembered husky voice, "but I didn't want to come between you and Jean Harlow." She reached up one narrow hand, and he took it gladly and pulled her to her feet. She could hardly weigh more than a hundred pounds. He realized that her hand was hot as he let go of it.

"And hello," she said.

She was wearing jeans and a gray sweatshirt again, or still. At least they were dry. Sydney caught again the scent of pears and cumin.

He was grinning too. Most of the books he sold he got from thrift stores and online used-book sellers, and these recent trips to Book City had been a self-respect excuse to keep looking for her here.

He groped for something to say. "I thought I found your 'Heroic' the other day," he told her.

She cocked her head, still smiling. The sweatshirt was baggy, but somehow she seemed to be flat-chested today. "You were looking for me?" she asked.

"I—guess I was. This was a closed-down motel, though, south of Santa Monica." He laughed self-consciously. "The sign says blank-R-O-blank-I-C. Eroic, see? It was originally Tropic, I gather."

Her green eyes had narrowed as he spoke, and it occurred to him that the condemned motel might actually be the place she'd referred to a couple of weeks earlier, and that she had not expected him to find it. "Probably it originally said 'erotic,'" she said lightly, taking his hand and stepping away from the Gregory Peck square. "Have you got a cigarette?"

"Yes." He pulled a pack of Camels and a lighter from his shirt pocket, and when she had tucked a cigarette between her lips—he noticed that she was not wearing lipstick today—he cupped his hand around the lighter and held the flame toward her. She held his hand to steady it as she puffed the cigarette alight.

"There couldn't be a motel called Erotic," he said.

"Sure there could, lover. To avoid complications."

"I'm George," he said. "What's your name?"

She shook her head, grinning up at him.

The bearded balloon man had shuffled across the pavement to them, deftly weaving a sort of bowler hat shape out of several long green balloons, and now he reached out and set it on her head.

"No, thank you," she said, taking it off and holding it toward the man, but he backed away, smiling through his beard and nodding. She stuck it onto the head of a little boy who was scampering past.

The balloon man stepped forward again and this time he snatched the cigarette from her mouth. "This is California, sister," he said, dropping it and stepping on it. "We don't smoke here."

"You should," she said, "it'd help you lose weight." She took Sydney's arm and started toward the sidewalk.

The balloon man called after them, "It's customary to give a gratuity for the balloons!"

"Get it from that kid," said Sydney over his shoulder.

The bearded man was pointing after them and saying loudly, "Tacky people, tacky people!"

"Could I have another cigarette?" she said as they stepped around the forecourt wall out of the shadows and started down the sunlit sidewalk toward the soft-drink and jewelry stands on the wider pavement in front of the Kodak Theater.

"Sure," said Sydney, pulling the pack and lighter out again. "Would you like a Coke or something?" he added, waving toward the nearest vendor. Their shadows stretched for yards ahead of them, but the day was still hot.

"I'd like a drink drink." She paused to take a cigarette, and again she put her hand over his as he lit it for her. "Drink, that knits up the raveled sleeve of care," she said through smoke as they started forward again. "I bet you know where we could find a bar."

"I bet I do," he agreed. "Why don't you want to tell me your name?"

"I'm shy," she said. "What did the Michelin Man say, when we were leaving?"

"He said, 'tacky people.'"

She stopped and turned to look back, and for a moment Sydney was afraid she intended to march back and cause a scene; but a moment later she had grabbed his arm and resumed their eastward course.

He could feel that she was shaking, and he peered back over his shoulder.

Everyone on the pavement behind them seemed to be couples moving away or across his view, except for one silhouetted figure standing a hundred feet back—it was an elderly white-haired woman in a shapeless dress, and he couldn't see if she was looking after them or not.

The girl had released his arm and taken two steps ahead, and he started toward her—

—and she disappeared.

Sydney rocked to a halt.

He had been looking directly at her in the bright afternoon sunlight. She had not stepped into a store doorway or run on ahead or ducked behind him. She had been occupying volume four feet ahead of him, casting a shadow, and suddenly she was not.

A bus that had been grinding past

on the far side of the parking meters to his right was still grinding past.

Her cigarette was rolling on the sidewalk, still lit.

She had not been a hallucination, and he had not experienced some kind of blackout.

Are you always so nice to dead people?

He was shivering in the sunlight, and he stepped back to half-sit against the rim of a black iron trash can by the curb. No sudden moves, he thought.

Was she a ghost? Probably, probably! What else?

Well then, you've seen a ghost, he told himself, that's all. People see ghosts. The balloon man saw her too—he told her not to smoke.

You fell in love with a ghost, that's all. People have probably done that.

He waited several minutes, gripping

the iron rim of the trash can and glancing in all directions, but she didn't reappear.

At last he was able to push away from the trash can and walk on, unsteadily, toward Book City; that had been his plan before he had met her again today, and nothing else seemed appropriate. Breathing wasn't difficult, but for at least a little while it would be a conscious action, like putting one foot in front of the other.

He wondered if he would meet her again, knowing that she was a ghost. He wondered if he would be afraid of her now. He thought he probably would be, but he hoped he would see her again anyway.

The quiet aisles of the book store, with the almost-vanilla scent of old paper, distanced him from the event on the sidewalk. This was his familiar world, as if all used book stores were actually one enormous magical building that you could enter through different doorways in Long Beach or Portland or Albuquerque. Always, reliably, there were the books with no spines that you had to pull out and identify, and the dust jackets that had to be checked for the dismissive words *Book Club Edition*, and the poetry section to be scanned for possibly underpriced Nora May French or George Sterling.

The shaking of his hands, and the disorientation that was like a half-second delay in his comprehension, were no worse than a hangover, and he was familiar with hangovers—the cure was a couple of drinks, and he would take the cure as soon as he got back to his apartment. In the meantime he was gratefully able to concentrate on the books, and within half an hour he had found several P. G. Wodehouse novels that he'd be able to sell for more than the prices they were marked at, and a clean five-dollar hardcover copy of Sabatini's *Bellarion*.

My books, he thought, and my poetry.

In the poetry section he found several signed Don Blanding books, but in his experience every Don Blanding book was signed. Then he found a first edition copy of Cheyenne Fleming's 1968 *More Poems*, but it was priced at twenty dollars, which was about the most it would ever go for. He looked on the title page for an inscription, but there wasn't one, and then flipped through the pages—and glimpsed handwriting.

He found the page again, and saw the name *Cheyenne Fleming* scrawled below one of the sonnets; and beside it was a thumb-print in the same fountain-pen ink.

If this was a genuine Fleming signature, the book was worth about two hundred dollars. He was familiar with her poetry, but he didn't think he'd ever seen her signature; certainly he didn't have any signed Flemings at home to compare this against. But Christine would probably be able to say whether it was real or not—Christine Dunn was a book dealer he'd sometimes gone in with on substantial buys.

He'd risk the twenty dollars and call her when he got back to his apartment. And just for today he would walk straight north to Franklin, not west on Hollywood Boulevard. Not quite yet, not this evening.

His apartment building was on Franklin just west of Highland, a jacaranda-shaded old two-storey horseshoe around an overgrown central courtyard, and supposedly Marlon Brando had stayed there before he'd become successful. Sydney's apartment was upstairs, and he locked the door after he had let himself into the curtained, tobacco-scented living room.

He poured himself a glass of bourbon from the bottle on the top kitchen shelf, and pulled a Coors from the refrigerator to chase the warm liquor with, and then he took his shopping bag to the shabby brown-leather chair in the corner and switched on the lamp.

It was of course the Fleming that interested him. He flipped open the book to the page with Fleming's name inked on it.

He recognized the sonnet from the first line—it was the rude sonnet to her sister…the sister who, he recalled, had become Fleming's literary executor after Fleming's suicide. Ironic.

He read the first eight lines of the sonnet, his gaze only bouncing over the lines since he had read it many times before:

To My Sister

Rebecca, if your mirror were to show
My face to you instead of yours, I wonder
If you would notice right away, or know
The vain pretense you've chosen to live under.
If ever phone or doorbell rang, and then
I heard your voice conversing, what you'd say
Would be what I have said, recalled again,
And I might sit in silence through the day.

Then he frowned and took a careful sip of the bourbon. The last six lines weren't quite as he remembered them:

But when the Resurrection Man shall bring
The moon to free me from these yellowed
    pages,
The gift is mine, there won't be anything
For you—and you can rest through all
    the ages

Under a stone that bears the cherished name
You thought should make the two of us
the same.

He picked up the telephone and punched in Christine's number.

After three rings he heard her say, briskly, "Dunn Books."

"Christine," he said, "George—uh—here." It was the first time he had spoken since seeing the girl disappear, and his voice had cracked. He cleared his throat and took a deep breath and let it out.

"Drunk again," said Christine.

"Again?" he said. "Still. Listen, I've got a first here of Fleming's *More Poems*, no dust-jacket but it's got her name written below one of the poems. Do you have a signed Fleming I could compare it with?"

"You're in luck, an e-Bay customer backed out of a deal. It's a *More Poems*, too."

"Have you got it right there?"

"Yeah, but what, you want me to describe her signature over the phone? We should meet at the Biltmore tomorrow, bring our copies."

"Good idea, and if this is real I'll buy lunch. But could you flip to the sonnet 'To My Sister'?"

"One second." A few moments later she was back on the phone. "Okay, what about it?"

"How does the sestet go?"

"It says, '*But when the daylight of the future shows/ The forms freed by erosion from their cages,/ It will be mine that quickens, gladly grows,/ And lives; and you can rest through all the ages/ Under a stone that bears the cherished name/ You thought should make the two of us the same.'* Bitter poem!"

Those were the familiar lines—the way the poem was supposed to go.

"Why," asked Christine, "is yours missing the bottom of the page?"

"No—I've—my copy has a partly different sestet." He read to her the last six lines on the page of the book he held. "Printed just like every other poem in the book, same type-face and all."

"Wow. Otherwise a standard copy of the first edition?"

"To the best of my knowledge, I don't know," he said, quoting a treasured remark from a bookseller they both knew. He added, "We'll know tomorrow."

"Eleven, okay? And take care of it—it might be worth wholesaling to one of the big-ticket dealers."

"I wasn't going to use it for a coaster. See you at eleven."

He hung up the phone, and before putting the book aside he touched the ink thumb-print beside the signature on the page. The paper wasn't warm or cold, but he shivered—this was a touch across decades. When had Fleming killed herself?

He got up and crossed the old carpets to the computer and turned it on, and as the monitor screen showed the Hewlett Packard logo and then the Windows background, he couldn't shake the mental image of trying to catch a woman's hand to keep her from falling into some abyss and only managing to brush her outstretched hand with one finger.

He typed in the address for Google—*sounds like a Chinaman trying to say something*—and then typed "cheyenne fleming," and when a list of sites appeared he clicked on the top one. He had a dial-up AOL connection, so the text appeared first, flanking a square where a picture would soon appear.

Cheyenne Fleming, he read, had been born in Hollywood in 1934, and had lived there all her life with her younger sister Rebecca. Both had gone to UCLA, Cheyenne with more distinction than Rebecca, and both had published books of poetry, though Rebecca's had always been compared unfavorably with Cheyenne's. The sisters apparently both loved and resented each other, and the article quoted several lines from the "To My Sister" sonnet—the version Christine had read to him over the phone, not the version in his copy of *More Poems*. Cheyenne

Fleming had shot herself in 1969, reportedly because Rebecca had stolen away her fiance. Rebecca became her literary executor.

At last the picture appeared on the screen—it was black and white, but Sydney recognized the thin face with its narrow eyes and wide humorous mouth, and he knew that the disordered hair would be red in a color photograph.

The tip of his finger was numb where he had touched her thumb-print.

I'm Shy, she had said. He had thought she was evading giving him her name. Shy for Cheyenne, of course. Pronounced Shy-*Ann*.

He glanced fearfully at his front door—what if she was standing on the landing out there right now, in the dusk shadows? He realized, with a shudder that made him carry his glass back to

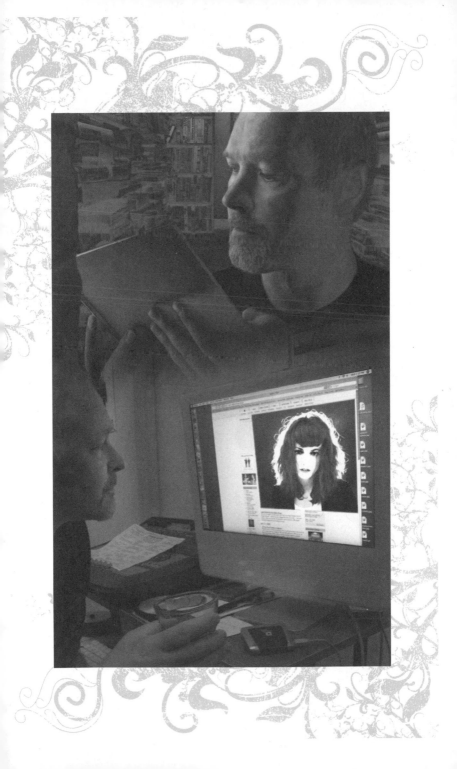

the kitchen for a re-fill, that he would open the door if she was—yes, and invite her in, invite her across his threshold. I finally fall in love, he thought, and it's with a dead woman. A suicide.

A line of black ants had found the coffee cup he'd left unwashed this morning, but he couldn't kill them right now.

Once his glass was filled again, he went to the living room window instead of the door, and he pulled the curtains aside. A huge orange full moon hung in the darkening sky behind the old TV antennas on the opposite roof. He looked down, but didn't see her among the shadowed trees and vines.

And in a Windingsheet of Vineleaf wrapped,

So bury me by some sweet Gardenside.

He closed the curtain and fetched the bottle and the twelve-pack of Coors to set beside his chair, then settled down to lose himself in one of the P. G. Wodehouse novels until he should be drunk enough to stumble to bed and fall instantly asleep.

As he trudged across Pershing Square from the parking structure on Hill Street toward the three imposing brown brick towers of the Biltmore Hotel, Sydney's squinting gaze kept being drawn in the direction of the new bright-yellow building on the south side of the square. His eyes were watering in the morning sun-glare anyway, and he wondered irritably why somebody would paint a new building in that idiotic kindergarten color.

He had awakened early, and his hangover seemed to be just a continuation of his disorientation from the day before. He had decided that he couldn't sell the Fleming book. Even though he had met her two weeks before finding the book, he was certain that the book was somehow his link to her.

Christine would be disappointed— part of the fun of bookselling was writing catalogue copy for extraordinary items, and she would have wanted to collaborate in the description of this item—but he couldn't help that.

His gaze was drawn again toward the yellow building, but now that he was closer to it he could see that it wasn't the building that his eyes had been drawn toward, but a stairway and pool just this side of it. Two six-foot brown stone spheres were mounted on the pool coping.

And he saw her sitting down there, on the shady side of one of the giant stone balls.

He was smiling and stepping across the pavement in that direction even before he was sure it was her, and the memory, only momentarily delayed, of who she must be didn't slow his pace.

She was wearing the jeans and sweatshirt again, and she stood up and waved at him when he was still a hundred feet away, and even at this distance he was sure he caught her pears-and-cumin scent.

He sprinted the last few yards, and her arms were wide so he hugged her when they met.

"George," she said breathily in his ear. The fruit-and-spice smell was strong.

"Shy," he said, and hugged her more tightly. He could feel her breastbone against his, and he wondered if she had been wearing a padded bra when he had first seen her. Then he held her by her shoulders at arm's length and smiled into her squinting, elfin eyes. "I've got to make a call," he said.

He pulled his cell phone out of his jacket pocket, flipped it open and tapped in Christine's well-remembered number. He was already ten minutes late for their meeting.

"Christine," he said, "I've got to beg off…no, I'm not going to be home. I'm going to be in Orange County—"

Cheyenne mouthed *Overnight*.

"—overnight," Sydney went on, "till tomorrow. No, I…I'll explain it later, and I owe you a lunch. No, I haven't sold it yet! I gotta run, I'm in traffic and I can't drive and talk at the same time. Right, right—'bye!"

He folded it and tucked it back into his pocket.

Cheyenne nodded. "To avoid complications," she said.

Sydney had stepped back from her, but he was holding her hand—possibly to keep her from disappearing again. "My New Year's resolution," he said with a rueful smile, "was not to tell any lies."

"My attitude toward New Year's resolutions is the same as Oscar Wilde's," she said, stepping around the pool coping and swinging his hand.

"What did he say about them?" asked Sydney, falling into step beside her.

"I don't know if he ever said anything

about them," she said, "but if he did, I'm sure I agree with it."

She looked back at him, then glanced past him and lost her smile.

"Don't turn around," she said quickly, so he just stared at her face, which seemed bony and starved between the wings of tangled red hair. "Now look around, but scan the whole square, like you're calculating if they could land the Goodyear blimp here."

Sydney let his gaze swivel from Hill Street, across the trees and broad pavement of the square, to the pillared arch of the Biltmore entrance. Up there toward the east end of the square he had seen a gray-haired woman in a loose blue dress; she seemed to be the same woman he had seen behind them on Hollywood Boulevard yesterday.

He let his eyes come back around to focus on Cheyenne's face.

"You saw that woman?" she said to him. "The one that looks like…some kind of featherless monkey? Stay away from her, she'll tell you lies about me."

Looking at the Biltmore entrance had reminded him that Christine might have parked in the Hill Street lot too. "Let's sit behind one of these balls," he said. And when they had walked down the steps and sat on the cement coping, leaning back against the receding under-curve of the nearest stone sphere, he said, "I found your book. I hope you don't mind that I know who you are."

She was still holding his hand, and now she squeezed it. "Who am I, lover?"

"You're Cheyenne Fleming. You— you're—"

"Yes. How did I die?"

He took a deep breath. "You killed yourself."

"I did? Why?"

"Because your sister—I read—ran off with your fiance."

She closed her eyes and twined her fingers through his. "Urban legends. Can I come over to your place tonight? I want to copy one of my poems in the book, write it out again in the blank space around the printed version, and I need you to hold my hand, guide my hand while I write it."

"Okay," he said. His heart was thudding in his chest. Inviting her over my threshold, he thought. "I'd like that," he added with dizzy bravado.

"I've got the pen to use," she went on. "It's my special pen, they buried me with it."

"Okay." Buried her with it, he thought. Buried her with it.

"I love you," she said, her eyes still closed. "Do you love me? Tell me you love me."

He was sitting down, but his head was spinning with vertigo as if an infinite black gulf yawned at his feet. This was her inviting *him* over *her* threshold.

"Under," he said in a shaky voice, "normal circumstances, I'd certainly be in love with you."

"Nobody falls in love under *normal* circumstances," she said softly, rubbing his finger with her warm thumb. He restrained an impulse to look to see if there was still ink on it. "Love isn't in the category of normal things. Not any worthwhile kind of love, anyway." She opened her eyes and waved her free hand behind them toward the square. "Normal people. I hate them."

"Me too," said Sydney.

"Actually," she said, looking down at their linked hands, "I didn't kill myself." She paused for so long that he was about to ask her what had happened, when she went on quietly, "My sister Rebecca shot me, and made it look like a suicide. After that she apparently *did* go away with my fiance. But she killed me because she had made herself into an imitation of me, and without me in the picture, *she'd* be the original." Through her hand he felt her shiver. "I've been alone in the dark for a long time," she said in a small voice.

Sydney freed his hand so that he could put his arm around her narrow shoulders, and he kissed her hair.

Cheyenne looked up with a grin that made slits of her eyes. "But I don't think she's prospered! Doesn't she look *terrible?*"

Sydney resisted the impulse to look around again. "Was that—"

Cheyenne frowned. "I've got to go—I can't stay here for very long at a time, not until we copy that poem."

She kissed him, and their mouths opened, and for a moment his tongue touched hers. When their lips parted their foreheads were pressed together, and he whispered, "Let's get that poem copied, then."

She smiled, deepening the lines in her cheeks, and looked down. "Sit back now and look away from me," she said. "And I'll come to your place tonight."

He pressed his palms against the surface of the cement coping and pushed himself away from her, and looked toward Hill Street.

After a moment, "Shy?" he said; and when he looked around she was gone. "I love you," he said to the empty air.

"Everybody did," came a raspy voice from behind and above him.

For a moment he went on staring at the place where Cheyenne had sat; then he sighed deeply and looked around.

The old woman in the blue dress was standing at the top of the stairs, and now began stepping carefully down them in boxy old-lady shoes.

Her eyes were pouchy above round cheeks and not much of a chin, and Sydney imagined she'd been cute decades ago.

"Are," he said in a voice he made himself keep level, "you Rebecca?"

She stopped in front of him and

nodded, frowning in the sun-glare. "Rebecca Fleming," she said. "The cherished name." The diesel-scented breeze was blowing her white hair around her face, and she pushed it back with one frail, spotted hand. "Did she say I killed her?"

After a moment's hesitation, "Yes," Sydney said.

She sat down, far enough away from him that he didn't feel called on to move further away. Why hadn't he brought a flask?

"True," she said, exhaling as if she'd been holding her breath. "True, I did." She looked across at him, and he reluctantly met her eyes. They were green, just like Cheyenne's.

"I bet," she said, "you bought a book of hers, signed." She barked two syllables of a laugh. "And I bet she's still got her fountain pen. We buried it with her."

"I don't think you and I have much to say to each other," said Sydney stiffly. He started to get to his feet.

"It was self-defense, if you're curious," she said, not stirring.

He paused, bracing himself on his hands.

"She came into my room," said Rebecca, "with a revolver. I woke up when she touched the cold muzzle to my forehead. This is thirty-seven years ago, but I remember it as if it were last night—we were in a crummy motel south of Santa Monica Boulevard, on one of her low-life tours. I sat up and pushed the gun away, but she kept trying to get it aimed at me—she was laughing, irritated, cajoling, I wasn't playing along properly—and when I pushed it back toward her it went off. Under her chin. I wrote a suicide note for her."

The old woman's face was stony. Sydney sat back down.

"I loved her," she said. "If I'd known that resisting her would end up killing her, I swear, I wouldn't have resisted." She smiled at him belligerently. "Crush an ant sometime, and then smell your fingers. I wonder what became of the clothes we buried her in. Not a sweat-shirt and jeans."

"A black linen suit," said Sydney, "with a white blouse. They were damp."

"Well, ground-water, you know, even with a cement grave-liner. And a padded bra, for the photographs. I fixed it up myself, crying so hard I could barely see the stitches—I filled the lining with bird-seed to flesh her out."

Sydney recalled the vines that had seemed to be embroidered on Cheyenne's bra, that first day. "It sprouted."

Rebecca laughed softly. "'Quickens, gladly grows.' She wants something from you." Rebecca fumbled in a pocket of her skirt. "Bring the moon to free her from these yellowed pages."

Sydney squinted at her. "You've read that version of the sonnet?"

Rebecca was now holding out a two-inch clear plastic cylinder with metal bands on it. "I was there when she wrote it. She read it to me when the ink was still wet. It was printed that way in only one copy of the book, the copy you obviously found, God help us all. This is one of her ink cartridges. You stick this end in the ink bottle and twist the other end—that retracts the plunger. When she was writing poetry she used to use about nine parts Schaeffer's black ink and one part her own blood."

She was still holding it toward him, so he took it from her.

"The signature in your book certainly contains some of her blood," Rebecca said.

"A signature and a thumbprint," said Sydney absently, rolling the narrow cylinder in his palm. He twisted the back end, and saw the tiny red ring of the plunger move smoothly up the inside of the clear barrel.

"And you touched the thumbprint."

"Yes. I'm glad I did."

"You brought her to this cycle of the moon. She arrived on the new moon, though you probably didn't find the book and touch her thumb till further on in the cycle; she'd instantly stain the whole twenty-eight days, I'm sure, backward and forward. Do you know yet what she wants you to do?"

If I'd known, Rebecca had said, *that resisting her would end up killing her, I swear, I wouldn't have resisted.* Sydney realized, to his dismay, that he believed her.

"Hold her hand, guide it, I guess, while she copies a poem," he said.

"*That* poem, I have no doubt. She's a ghost—I suppose she imagines that writing it again will project her spirit back to the night when she originally wrote it—so she can make a better attempt at killing me three years later, in 1969. She was thirty-five, in '69. I was thirty-three."

"She looks younger."

"She always did. See little Shy riding horseback, you'd think she was twelve years old." Rebecca sat back. "She's pretty physical, right? I mean, she can hold things, touch things?"

Sydney remembered Cheyenne's fingers intertwined with his.

"Yes."

"I'd think she could hold a pen. I wonder why she needs help copying the poem."

"I—" Sydney began.

But Rebecca interrupted him. "If you do it for her," she said, "and it works, she won't have died. I'll be the one that died in '69. She'll be seventy-two now, and you won't have met her. Well, she'll probably look you up, if she remembers to be grateful, but you won't remember any of…this interlude with her." She smiled wryly. "And you certainly won't meet me. That's a plus, I imagine. Do you have any high-proof liquor, at your house?"

"You can't come over!" said Sydney, appalled.

"No, I wasn't thinking of that. Never mind. But you might ask her—"

She had paused, and Sydney raised his eyebrows.

"You might ask her not to kill me, when she gets back there. I know I'd have left, moved out, if she had told me she really needed that. I'd have stopped...trying to be her. I only did it because I loved her." She smiled, and for a moment as she stood up Sydney could see that she must once have been very pretty.

"Goodbye, Resurrection Man," she said, and turned and shuffled away up the cement steps.

Sydney didn't call after her. After a moment he realized that he was still holding the plastic ink-cartridge, and he put it in his pocket.

High-proof liquor, he thought unhappily.

Back in his apartment after making a couple of purchases, he poured himself a shot of bourbon from the kitchen bottle and sat down by the window with the Fleming book.

*But when the Resurrection Man shall
    bring
The moon to free me from these yellowed
    pages,*

*The gift is mine, there won't be anything
For you.*

The moon had been full last night.
Or maybe just a hair short of full, and it
would be full tonight.

*You might ask her not to kill me, when
she gets back there.*

He opened the bags he had carried
home from a liquor store and a stationer's,
and he pulled the ink cartridge out of
his pocket.

One bag contained a squat glass
bottle of Schaeffer's black ink, and he
unscrewed the lid; there was a little
pool of ink in the well on the inside of
the open bottle's rim, and he stuck the
end of the cartridge into the ink and

twisted the back. The plunger retracted, and the barrel ahead of it was black.

When it was a third filled, he stopped, and he opened the other bag. It contained a tiny plastic 50-milliliter bottle—what he thought of as breakfast-sized—of Bacardi 151-proof rum. He unscrewed the cap and stuck the cartridge into the vapory liquor. He twisted the end of the cartridge until it stopped, filled, and even though the cylinder now contained two-thirds rum, it was still jet-black.

He had considered buying lighter-fluid, but decided that the 151-proof rum—seventy-five percent alcohol— would probably be more flammable. And he could drink what he didn't use.

He was dozing in the chair when he heard someone moving in the kitchen. He sat up, disoriented, and hoarsely called, "Who's there?"

He lurched to his feet, catching the book but missing the tiny empty rum bottle.

"Who were you expecting, lover?" came Cheyenne's husky voice. "Should I have knocked? You already invited me."

He stumbled across the dim living room into the kitchen. The overhead light was on in there, and through the little kitchen window he saw that it was dark outside.

Cheyenne was sweeping the last of the ants off the counter with her hand, and as he watched she rubbed them vigorously between her palms and wiped her open hands along her jaw

and neck, then picked up the half-full bourbon bottle.

She was wearing the black linen skirt and jacket again—and, he could see, the birdseed-sprouting bra under the white blouse. The clothes were somehow still damp.

"I talked to Rebecca," he blurted, thinking about the ink cartridge in his pocket.

"I told you not to," she said absently. "Where do you keep glasses? Or do you expect me to drink right out of the bottle? Did she say she killed me in self-defense?"

"Yes."

"Glasses?"

He stepped past her and opened a cupboard and handed her an Old-Fashioned glass. "Yes," he said again.

She smiled up at him from beneath

her dark eyelashes as she poured a couple of ounces of amber liquor into the glass, then put down the bottle and caressed his cheek. The fruit-and-spice smell of crushed ants was strong.

"It was my fault!" she said, laughing as she spoke. "I shouldn't have touched her with the barrel! And so it was little Shy that wound up getting killed, *miserable dictu!* I was…*nonplussed* in eternity." She took a deep sip of the bourbon and then sang, "'Take my hand, I'm nonplussed in eternity…'"

He wasn't smiling, so she pushed out her thin red lips. "Oh, lover, don't pout. Am I my sister's keeper? Did you know she claimed I got my best poems by stealing her ideas? As if anybody couldn't tell from reading *her* poetry which of us was the original! At least I had already got that copy of my book out there, out in the world, like a message in a bottle, a soul in a bottle, for you to eventually—"

Sydney had held up his hand, and she stopped. "She said to tell you...not to kill her. She said she'd just move out if you asked her to. If she knew it was important to you."

She shrugged. "Maybe."

He frowned and took a breath, but she spoke again before he could.

"Are you still going to help me copy out my poem? I can't write it by myself, because the first word of it is the name of the person who killed me."

Her eyes were wide and her eyebrows were raised as she looked down at the book in his hand and then back up at him.

"I'd do it for you," she added softly, "because I love you. Do you love me?"

She couldn't be taller than five-foot one inch, and with her long neck and thin arms, and her big eyes under the disordered hair, she looked young and frail.

"Yes," he said. I do, he thought. And I'm going to exorcise you. I'm going to spread that flammable ink-and-rum mix over the page and then touch it with a cigarette.

It was printed that way in only one copy of the book, Rebecca had said, *the copy you obviously found, God help us all.* A soul in a bottle.

There won't be another Resurrection Man.

He made himself smile. "You've got a pen, you said."

She reached thin fingers into the neck of her blouse and pulled out a long, tapering black pen. She shook it to dislodge a thin white tendril with a tiny green leaf on it.

"May I?" he asked, holding out his hand.

She hesitated, then laid the pen in his palm.

He handed her the book, then pulled off the pen's cap, exposing the gleaming, wedge-shaped nib. "Do you need to dip it in an ink bottle?" he asked.

"No, it's got a cartridge in it. Unscrew the end."

He twisted the barrel and the nib-end rotated away from the pen, and after a few more turns it came loose in his hand, exposing a duplicate of the ink-cartridge he had in his pocket.

"Pull the cartridge off," she said suddenly, "and lick the end of it. Didn't she tell you about my ink?"

"No," he said, his voice unsteady. "Tell me about your ink."

"Well, it's got a little bit of my blood in it, though it's mostly ink." She was flipping through the pages of the book. "But some blood. Lick it, the punctured end of the cartridge." She looked up at him and grinned. "As a chaser for the rum I smell on your breath."

For ten seconds he stared into her deep green eyes, then he raised the cartridge and ran his tongue across the end of it. He didn't taste anything.

"That's my dear man," she said, taking his hand and stepping onto the living room carpet. "Let's sit in that chair you were napping in."

As they crossed the living room, Sydney slid his free hand into his pocket and clasped the rum-and-ink cartridge next to the blood-and-ink one.

The one he had prepared this afternoon was up by his knuckles, the other at the base of his palm.

She let go of his hand to reach out and switch on the lamp, and Sydney pulled a pack of Camels out of his shirt pocket and shook one free.

"Sit down," she said, "I'll sit in your lap. I hardly weigh anything. Are there limits to what you'd do for someone you love?"

Sydney hooked a cigarette onto his lip and tossed the pack aside. "Limits?" he said as he sat down and clicked a lighter at the end of the cigarette. "I don't know," he said around a puff of smoke.

"I think you're not one of those normal people," she said.

"I hate 'em." He laid his cigarette in the smoking stand beside the chair.

"Me too," she said, and she slid onto his lap and curled her left arm around his shoulders. Her skirt and sleeve were damp, but not cold.

With her right hand she opened the book to the sonnet "To My Sister."

"Lots of margin space for us to write in," she said.

Her hot cheek was touching his, and when he turned to look at her he found that he was kissing her, gently at first and then passionately, for this moment not caring that her scent was the smell of crushed ants.

"Put the cartridge," she whispered into his mouth, "back into the pen and screw it closed."

He carefully fitted one of the cartridges into the pen and whirled the base until it was tight.

George Sydney stood up from crouching beside the shelf of cook-books, holding a copy of James Beard's *On Food*. It was his favorite of Beard's books, and if he couldn't sell it at a profit he'd happily keep it.

He hadn't found any other likely books here today, and now it was nearly noon and time to walk across the boulevard to Boardner's for a couple of quick drinks.

"There he is," said the man behind the counter and the cash register. "George, this lady has been coming in every day for the last week, looking for you."

Sydney blinked toward the brightly sunlit store windows, and in front of the counter he saw the silhouette of a short elderly woman with a halo of back-lit white hair.

He smiled and shuffled forward. "Well, hi," he said.

"Hello, George," she said in a husky voice, holding out her hand.

He stepped across the remaining distance and shook her hand. "What—" he began.

"I was just on my way to the Chinese Theater," she said. She was smiling up at him almost sadly, and though her face was deeply etched with wrinkles, her green eyes were lively and young. "I'm going to lay three pennies in the indentations in Gregory Peck's square."

He laughed in surprise. "I do that with Jean Harlow!"

"That's where I got the idea." She leaned forward and tipped her face up and kissed him briefly on the lips, and he dropped the James Beard book.

He crouched to retrieve the book, and when he straightened up she had already stepped out the door. He saw her walking away west down Hollywood Boulevard, her white hair fluttering around her head in the wind.

The man behind the counter was middle-aged, with a graying moustache. "Do you know who your admirer is, George?" he asked with a kinked smile.

Sydney had taken a step toward the door, but some misgiving made him stop. He exhaled to clear his head of a sharp sweet, musty scent.

"Uh," he said distractedly, "no. Who is she?"

"That was Cheyenne Fleming. I got her to sign some copies of her books the other day, so I can double the prices."

"I thought she was dead by now." Sydney tried to remember what he'd read about Fleming. "When was it she got paroled?"

"I don't know. In the '80s? Some time after the death penalty was repealed in the '70s, anyway." He waved at a stack of half a dozen slim dark books on the desk behind him. "You want one of the signed ones? I'll let you have it for the original price, since she only came in here looking for you."

Sydney looked at the stack.

"Nah," he said, pushing the James Beard across the counter. "Just this."

A few moments later he was outside on the brass-starred sidewalk, squinting after Cheyenne Fleming. He could see her, a hundred feet away to the west now, striding away.

He rubbed his face, trying to get rid

of the odd scent. And as he walked away, east, he wondered why that kiss should have left him feeling dirty, as if it had been a mortal sin for which he couldn't now phrase the need for absolution.